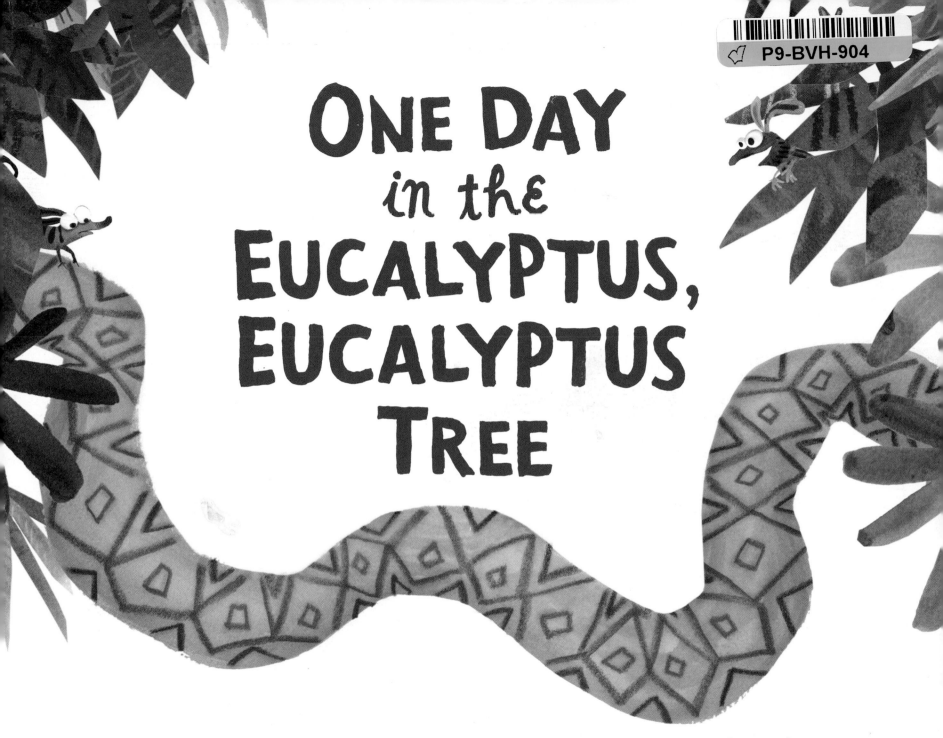

# One Day in the Eucalyptus, Eucalyptus Tree

Story by Daniel Bernstrom ✾ Pictures by Brendan Wenzel

SCHOLASTIC INC.

One day in the leaves
of the eucalyptus tree
hung a scare in the air
where no eye could see,

EUCALYPTUS

when along **skipped** a boy
with a whirly-twirly toy,
to the shade of the eucalyptus,
eucalyptus tree.

**Down,
down**

slid the
snake

from the leaves
of the tree

and **gobbled** up the boy
with his whirly-twirly toy,

one day in the **eucalyptus,
eucalyptus** tree.

"I'll bet," said the boy,
in the belly dark and deep,
"that you're still very hungry
and there's more you can eat."

"Do you think," said the snake
to the boy with the toy,
"that there's room for something **yummy**
with you inside my tummy?"

**Cheep, cheep** came a chirp
from the leaves of the tree.

Oh! A bird with a worm in
a game of hide-and-seek.

Sneaky-slidey **zipped** the snake
from his place in the leaves

and **gobbled** up the bird
and her ooey-gooey worm,

one day in the **eucalyptus**,
**eucalyptus** tree.

"I'll bet," said the boy,
in the belly dark and deep,
"that you're still very hungry,
and there's more you can eat."

**Purr, purr** came a stir from the leaves of the tree.

Oh! A cat in a nap on his furry, furry back.

Under-over slid the snake
from his place in the leaves
and **gobbled** up the cat
in his dozy-cozy nap,

one day in the **eucalyptus**,
**eucalyptus** tree.

"Oh surely, very surely,
Mr. Snake," said the boy,
"there is room. Still more room.
So much more to enjoy!"

**Crinkle, wrinkle** came a rustle from the leaves of the tree.

Oh! A sloth cloaked in moss, sipping leafy, leafy tea.

**Wiggle-waggle** stretched the snake from his place in the leaves and **gobbled** up the sloth clothed in fuzzy-wuzzy moss,

one day in the **eucalyptus, eucalyptus** tree.

"I'll bet," said the boy,
in the belly dark and deep,
"that you're still very hungry,
that there's more you can eat."

**Slurp, buuuuurrrrp!** came a belch from the leaves of the tree.

Oh! An ape eating grapes, lounging like a queen.

**Twist-twist** bent the snake from his place in the leaves

and **gobbled** up the ape and her munchy bunch of grapes,

one day in the **eucalyptus**, **eucalyptus** tree.

"Oh surely, very surely,
Mr. Snake," said the boy,
"there is room. Still more room.
So much more to enjoy!"

**Munch, munch** came a crunch from the leaves of the tree. Oh! A rare kind of bear munching tasty, tasty greens.

**Up, up** snaked the snake from his place in the leaves and **gobbled** up the bear with the qually-wally hair, one day in the **eucalyptus**, **eucalyptus** tree.

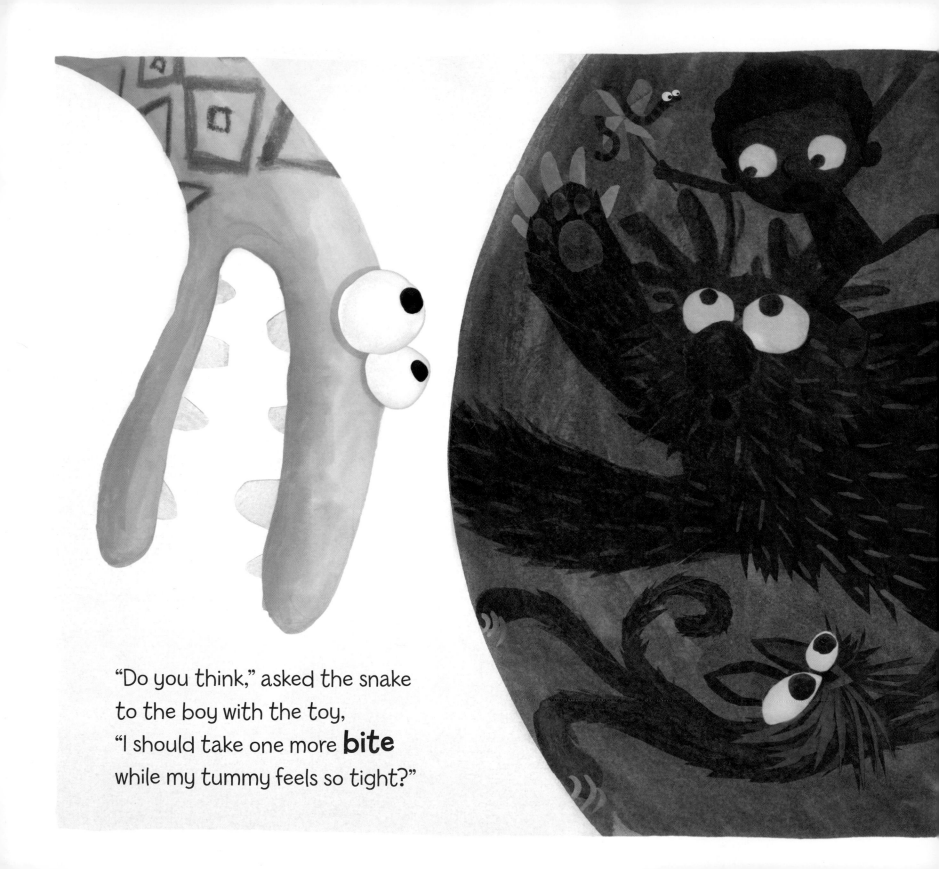

"Do you think," asked the snake
to the boy with the toy,
"I should take one more **bite**
while my tummy feels so tight?"

"Oh surely, very surely,
Mr. Snake," said the boy.
"There is room, so much room.
Go ahead, please enjoy!"

**Buzz, buzz** hummed a noise
from the leaves of the tree.
Oh! A hive full of bees,
 dancing happily.

**Creeky-eeky** inched the snake
from his place in the leaves
and **gobbled** up the hive
and the bumbling bees inside,

one day in the **eucalyptus**,
**eucalyptus** tree.

"I'll bet," said the boy,
in the belly dark and deep,
"that you're still very hungry,
that there's more you can eat."

"**No,**" said the snake.

"Oh surely, very surely, Mr. Snake,"
said the boy, "there is room.
Still more room . . ."

"**No,**" said the snake.

"Something small?" asked the boy.

**Sniff, sniff** hissed the snake
from his place in the leaves.

Oh! A fruit, a small fruit,
swaying in the breeze.
And on that piece of fruit,
that plummy-chummy fruit,

**Gurgle-gurgle** came a blurble
from that belly deep and full.

STRETCH!
# STRETCH!
# STRETCH!

BURP! BELCH!
BLAAAAAAAAAAAAAAAAAAAR!

Out **whizzed** the fly,
Out **rolled** the fruit,
Out **buzzed** the hive,
Out **ran** the bear,
Out **swung** the ape,
Out **slunk** the sloth,
Out **dashed** the cat,
Out **flew** the bird,
Out **slimed** the worm.

And out **skipped** the boy
with his whirly-twirly toy.

And . . .

"Ohhh," **moaned** the snake,
"I've a crummy tummyache."

One day in the **eucalyptus**,
**eucalyptus** tree.

To Laken and Hudson
—D.B.

For the Kopila kids
—B.W.

EUCALYPTUS

No part of this publication may be reproduced, stored in a retrieval system, or transmitted in any form or by any means, electronic, mechanical, photocopying, recording, or otherwise, without written permission of the publisher. For information regarding permission, write to Katherine Tegen Books, an imprint of HarperCollins Children's Books, a division of HarperCollins Publishers, 195 Broadway, New York, NY 10007 • ISBN 978-1-338-27376-2 • Text copyright © 2016 by Daniel Bernstrom. Illustrations copyright © 2016 by Brendan Wenzel. All rights reserved. Published by Scholastic Inc., 557 Broadway, New York, NY 10012, by arrangement with Katherine Tegen Books, an imprint of HarperCollins Children's Books, a division of HarperCollins Publishers. SCHOLASTIC and associated logos are trademarks and/or registered trademarks of Scholastic Inc. • The publisher does not have any control over and does not assume any responsibility for author or third-party websites or their content

12 11 10 9 8 7 6 5 4 3 2 1      18 19 20 21 22 23 • Printed in the U.S.A.      40 • This edition first printing, January 2018 • The artist used everything imaginable to create the digital illustrations for this book. • Typography by Rachel Zegar